To those who love
Glamour,
PARIS & PINK
this est pour vous.*
Fashion is Passion
any which way –
You need it, You breathe it,
don't care what you Pay!
and
to those who speak
"La Langue des Français"**
please don't dismay.
My French est mauvais,***
I call it "Faux French"****
Quite Fashionable today!

* (AY POOR VOO) Is for you
** (LA LONG DAY FRAHN-SAY) The French language
*** (AY MO-VAY) Is not the best
**** (FOE FRENCH) Fake French

Zat Cat!

*

A Haute Couture Tail

Chesley McLaren

scholastic press ✳ new york

LIBRARY OF CONGRESS CATALOGING-IN-PUBLICATION DATA

McLaren, Chesley. Zat Cat! A haute couture tail/ written and illustrated by Chesley McLaren.—1st ed. p. cm. Summary: A scruffy stray cat finds his life changed when he disrupts a Paris fashion show and unwittingly creates a new style that makes him the rage of Paris.

ISBN 0-439-27316-1 [1. Cats—Fiction. 2. Fashion shows —Fiction. 3. Paris (France)—Fiction. 4. France —Fiction. 5. Stories in rhyme.] PZ8.3.M2255 Cat 2002 [E]—dc21 2001020755 10 9 8 7 6 5 4 3 2 1 02 03 04 05 06 Printed in Singapore 46 First edition, March 2002

The display type was handlettered by Chesley McLaren. The text type was set in Fontesque. The illustrations in this book were painted in gouache. Book design by Marijka Kostiw

For Mum,

toujours dans mon cœur

et jamais deuxième!

And Dad,

Hayden, Harriet,

Monica, Brittany,

Rebecca, Sam,

Paxton, Chase,

and of course

Monsieur Etoile.

Merci, merci to Tracy Mack

and Marijka Kostiw

for bringing ZAT CAT! to life

and to Doug, je t'adore, mon amour!

He was born a fine cat in the heart of $\mathcal{P}aree,$ *

the youngest of six in his petite family.

* (PA-REE)
Paris, the most glamourous
city in the world

But his mischievous ways led him astray.

Now he roams about town,

down the **Champs Elysées**,*

and when the mood

strikes him,

he dines **au café**.**

*(SHAUM-ZAY-LEE-ZAY)
The most famous avenue in Paris
**(O CA-FAY)
At a place to meet and eat

*Jardin Luxembourg**

is his sunny day spot.

*(JAHR-DAN LUX-EM-BOORG)
A beautiful park—fit for a king

Le Musée du Louvre*

is the place when it's not.

* (LUH MOO-ZAY DOO LOOV-RUH)
A magnificent museum
bursting with treasures

Sometimes he resides

on a balcony or two . . .

but waking up early

just does not do!

Hotels, he finds,

are the absolute best

for a midnight guest's

luxurious rest.

Quite happy is he,

this scruffy stray cat . . .

. . . a little affection

is all that he lacks—

shopkeepers shoo him,

poodles

pooh-pooh

him.

And when he rubs up

against ladies at tea,

they scream out in horror

so he has to flee!

But then one day

après déjeuner,*

all of a sudden

while stealing a bite,

he happened upon

the most incredible sight.

The whole town started racing

down the **rue de Rivoli****

when someone yelled out,

"It's a quarter to three!"

Ladies with poodles, men in berets,

waiters and mothers ran from **cafés**.

* (AH-PRAY DAY-JOO-NAY)
After lunch
** (ROO DUH RIV-O-LEE)
A chic street in the heart of Paris

A huge crowd had gathered at a fancy hotel

(one that he knew exceptionally well).

Everyone was fighting and clamoring to see:

Le "wild & glamourous" de PAREE!*

C'est l'Œuvre Spectaculaire du Grand Couturier**

Monsieur Pierre.

Will it be le "show" du jour,***

haute couture**** as none before?

His new designs—

will they change the times?

*(LUH WILD AND GLA-MOOR-US DUH PA-REE)
What's wild and glamourous in Paris
**(SAY LUHVR SPEC-TAC-OO-LAIR
DOO GRAND COO-TOOR-EE-AY)
It's the fashion extravaganza of the master designer

***(LUH SHOW DOO JOOR)
The show of the day
****(OTE COO-TOOR)
Glamourous dresses
for the truly chic

He squeezed through the crowd.

But, cats not allowed!

"You miserable **chat**,* 'tis not **pour vous**,"**

and down the stairs he flew.

*(SHAH) Cat
**(POOR VOO) For you

During this bout,

the lights fade out,

a hush falls

over l'air.

Le Grand Salon

The music starts, the curtain parts,

and out strut three **mademoiselles*** so fair.

*(MA-DEM-WAH-ZEL)
The lovely girls of fashion

Such glitter, such style,

as they twirl down the aisle.

Brushing himself off with a swish of his tail,

he nudges the door but to no avail.

He scurries 'round back, leaping sill to sill,

so he too can glimpse the mysterious thrill.

Never has he seen such a dazzling sight—

flowers and fabrics and corsets sooo tight.

Before he can even
meow or blink,
    he's whisked off his feet
        by a sash in pink!

He flies through the air,
clawing hats and hair.

Ball gowns of satin
are shredded to bits.

Laces and ribbons totally ripped.

Baubles and bangles strewn on the floor,

the glorious flowers are no more.

Shrieks from the girls as they look on in terror.

"What will become of Monsieur from this error?"

Monsieur, we see, has taken to weeping.

Ten weeks of work,

not a bit worth keeping.

But the show must go on!

The music is thumping,

photographers jumping,

and the crowd is bursting to see . . .

what, oh what, will the finale be!?

so Soignée
au Courant
Chic, Chic, Chic

Whispers of wonder turn to roars of delight,

as our four-legged friend struts into the light.

So original, exotic, and free.

These ingenious designs

C'est la "Rage" de PAREE!*

One by one, they float out on

the stage . . .

Pour le Finale
beaucoup de Bijoux
beaucoup de PINK

"C'est la Rage de PAREE?"*

says Monsieur Pierre,

wiping his tears and smoothing his hair.

"Why zis terrible mess zat was a dress.

Zat **chat**, zat cat, where's he?"

By the tip of his tail,

under feet over rail,

he leaps to the street

tout de suite!**

*(SAY LA RAGE DUH PA-REE)
Are the hit of Paris
**(TOOT DUH SWEET)
Very quickly

Imagine his surprise

when met by the eyes

of Monsieur Pierre,

Le Grand Couturier.

A smile on his face,

a table with lace.

Mountains of cream.

Is this a dream?

Monsieur Pierre declares his admiration.

This scruffy stray cat made him the sensation!

For Monsieur Pierre became more famous that day

when his collection was hailed "Beyond *le Frais*."*

Frayed coats, frayed dresses, frayed anything at all.

He promises a home, a name of distinction,

love and affection, a life of purrr . . . fection.

*(BEE-OND LUH FRAY)
Priceless

He was named $\mathcal{E}toile$*

for his stardom glowed.

Even VOGUE declared him,

"$\mathcal{L}e$ $\mathcal{C}hat$ de $\mathcal{M}ode!$" **

*(AY-TWAL)
Star
**(LUH SHAH DUH MODE)
The Fashionable Cat

From Paris to London, New York and Milan,

the look of the moment is sure to live on!

For already in Paris women of style

are shredding their dresses and donning a smile.

Now every day après déjeuner Monsieur Étoile curls up in the sun dreaming of all the fun yet to come.